Presents
for Pipkin

ISBN 0 86112 582 7
© Brimax Books Ltd 1989
Published by Brimax Books Ltd, Newmarket, England 1989
Printed in Italy

Presents
for Pipkin

by Lucy Kincaid • Illustrated by Eric Kincaid

Brimax Books · Newmarket · England

Pipkin Rabbit is staying with his Grandma and Grandpa. They live in Long Grass Lane.

Grandpa is digging the potato patch.
Pipkin is helping.

Grandpa is hot. He takes off his hat.
"I can hold it for you, Grandpa," says Pipkin.

Pipkin puts the hat on. It is too big.
He can see his toes but that is all.

Now Pipkin tries to dig with Grandpa's shovel.
It is too heavy. He falls over.

Grandma and Grandpa have a surprise.
They give Pipkin two packages.

There is a hat inside one package.
There is a shovel inside the other package.

"Grandpa looks like a big Pipkin and Pipkin looks like a little Grandpa," laughs Grandma.

"Where shall I dig?" asks Pipkin.
"You can clear the weeds from
Grandma's flower bed," says Grandpa.

Grandpa is busy. He does not watch
what Pipkin is doing. Pipkin is busy too.

Weeds and flowers look the same to Pipkin.
He digs them all up.

"Oh dear!" says Grandpa, when he sees
what Pipkin has done.

"I was trying to help," sobs Pipkin.
"I know," says Grandpa, drying Pipkin's tears.

Grandpa sorts out the flowers and the weeds.
He puts the flowers back where they belong.

The flower bed is full of flowers again
but it is full of footprints too.

"We must clear those footprints away,"
says Grandpa. Grandpa lets Pipkin do it.

All the footprints are gone. Pipkin sees
Grandma coming. He hides in the long grass.

Grandpa tells Grandma what has happened.
"Oh dear!" says Grandma. She calls Pipkin.

"I am sorry, Grandma," says Pipkin.
"Please let me keep my shovel."

"Of course you can," says Grandma.
Pipkin is happy now. He gives Grandma
a big kiss.